Q.W.E.R.T.Y.

By Barbara Avon

Q.W.E.R.T.Y

Qwerty: A Haunting. Written by Barbara Avon

Facebook: @BarbaraAvonAuthor

Twitter: @barb_avon

Cover Design by Barbara Avon

Original Poem: "Intruder" circa 1997. Copyright: Barbara Avon

This is dedicated...

to the ones I love.

Intruder

Who is knocking at my door?

Will you knock forever more?

Will you be there in the morn?

Will you mend what I have torn?

Is your call silently true?

Or are your words your tool, are they your cue?

To torment, manipulate, lie and kill,

The one who loved you, and loves you still.

One

September, 1972

He thought of the (use grim?) reaper, gnashing his teeth into the flesh of the forgotten one. The one they left for dead, played dead, protecting herself from all of the wild creatures of the night. She was exposed, with naked flesh sparkling (change later) underneath the light of the moon. He was lurking somewhere, melding its shape with that of the trees. They (not clear, change) looked like humans standing above her, and staring down at her, ready to dissect her very soul from flesh, and skin and bones, exposing that which she feared most...

The red scribbles on the note pad reminded him of her blood as it filled her dimpled cheeks. He threw down his pen and stretched his long, lean body on the couch, with one arm draped over his scrunched green eyes. His eyes reminded her of a feline. Her mating call became a screech of sorts, inviting him to her lair. She would ravage his body in a world where time ceased to matter. Together, they would abandon themselves and seduce each other until their impure thoughts froze the moment for what it was. It was a covenant between them, etched invisibly in their wedding rings.

They had left the diner, floating on caffeine rushes and sugary highs, oblivious to heaven's tears that failed to permeate the moment with anything other than romantic nostalgia.

"Like the day you proposed, remember?" Her breath was

warm against his neck. They ran like children to their pickup, seeking its bed as if wrapping themselves in the warm, fluffy blankets at home. Naked and unashamed, they explored each other's bodies like virgins do, tentatively and with fear in each kiss. She revelled in her disembodiment and he watched her face morph into something wicked and unaffected by the flashes of light that skipped across the ink black sky. He dressed himself only long enough to prance across the parking lot to order something warm to drink, and soothe their throats that were parched by the sorts of sounds that lovers make. It was her father's store, and the kid at the register was aloof to Luke's bare torso and bare feet, wanting only to chew on his licorice and gaze into his sweetheart's eyes. As the semi crashed into the back of the old Ford, the kid's face changed, along with Claudia's crumpled, twisted torso, and Luke saw her name scripted in the electric current that danced above her, as if welcoming her home.

He had thrown his ring into the coffin, as onlookers tried to hide their embarrassment, and thought of gentler things like the bubbling pot of tomato sauce in their huge Italian kitchens. He commemorated their love with a bottle of whisky and a razor blade, marking his toned arms with exactly five slashes, one for each year of marital bliss. That night, masked behind an intoxicated version of himself, he drew a heart with his own blood on the bathroom mirror and his reflection humiliated him by trapping him in a state of self-induced solitude.

Family members left offerings on his doorstep of lasagna, torte, ragu, and clean underwear. The feral cats feasted on the fare and left the garments to rot until his neighbours came like thieves in the night to wipe the slate clean.

For a full year, Luke mourned, disparaging gifts, and accepting well intended slaps to the face by his ma who believed that she could shock him back to reality. At the one year mark, he picked up his pen, dedicating every single word to a rotted corpse, never getting past chapter 1.

TWO

Every word was like an agonizing grip to his heart. The letters were before his eyes, belittling his intelligence. They failed to string together in perfect order likening him to a disjointed acrobat, poised precariously on the trapeze, who would soon fall to his death.

The secret code resounding on the front door nudged him off the couch. It was the same code they used as kids when they would sneak out in the middle of the night and knock on each other's windows to debate over the finer sex, or relay stories of sex exploits gone awry, like the time Becky Grey bluffed rape. Her pastor had taken her into the confessional for hours, until her virginity became as obvious as the stained glass windows depicting Mother Mary.

Several seconds passed before he could open the door to a shorter, fatter version of himself.

"What the fuck is that?"

Ricky's straight brown locks dripped on his clean floor. He carried the old typewriter by resting it on both forearms.

"For you. Zia's going away present."

She died a spinster and all of her 98 lbs were celebrated today in her mansion on top of the hill with no name. The street sign was stolen a year ago and the city discarded the work order requesting a replacement, into a monstrous "to do" pile.

"That's all I get?"

He watched as Rick made himself at home by leaving soiled footprints on his way from the foyer to the living room.

"Better than what I got," Rick said, putting down the machine and shoving his hairy wrist towards his cousin to show off a cheap timepiece. "Doesn't even work."

Luke stood petrified at the open door. He looked outside, titling his head back and forth in tandem with the swaying trees where her voice rustled beneath the choir of the shaking leaves. He spat on the porch, mixing his saliva with the rain, and locked the door by securing several dead bolts as if trying to keep her out.

"Gotta smoke?"

He made his way back to the couch and thrust his chin towards the coffee table where the typewriter took up most of the space. It was a Remington, rusted on the sides and missing the "Q".

"How many fucking words begin with Q?"

"What?"

"Answer the question."

"You smokin' the good stuff again? Question is one. Queen, queer, quiet, quite...why the fuck you asking?"

"It's missing the Q. Someone pounded the fuck out of it. Where the hell you going already?"

Rick crushed out his smoke and stood, mostly so that his newly pressed pants wouldn't wrinkle.

"Got a date with Sandra."

"I thought you didn't like her."

"I didn't like her when I thought she didn't like me."

Luke pulled the machine towards himself. A yellowed sheet of paper sang to him: *Mary had a little lamb, little lamb, little lamb....*

"Little Elena was playing with it at the wake," Ricky told him, reading his jumbled mind. "Thanks for the smoke. You goin' to let me out of Fort Knox, or what?"

"The 'or what'."

"*Goddamn*, you really need to get laid. See you around."

He waited until he heard the door close before punching at the space where the "Q" should be.

q q q q q q q q q q q q q q q q q q...Why is this working? That is the question...

He stared at the letters, willing them to breathe. Scroll, Punch, punch, punch...

The queer queen went quite quiet...

"Good one, asshole..." he mumbled out loud, cursing Ricky.

He tried again:

They danced in the castle ballroom beneath gilded masks. A jester used words to paint smiles of mirth on the King and his queen. The midnight hour came and went. This was their world, until the morning dawn would see their enemies cross the moat, disguised beneath the same gilded masks... (maybe use later)

He plagiarized little Elena's words: *Mary had a little lamb, little lamb, little lamb...*

His niece had the same dark hair as him, and the same green eyes, framed beneath heavy brows. In a few years, she will pluck them, to make them more feminine and to attract the horny boys who won't give a rat's ass about her eyebrows. Her mother lacks the vein that leads to one's heart. His sister had tried to smother him when he was four years old, with her crusty, snotty pillow, claiming it was just a game. When Luke was old enough, he went around school telling everyone he was an only child. His father locked him in the fruit cellar all night when she tattled on him. She stood guard at the door, giggling and sucking on a lollipop, slurping like a stray, rabid bitch, lapping at a bowl of water.

He tore a blank sheet from his notepad, removed the ancient paper, and stuffed the new one in its place:

~~He...no, She...Fuck it...~~*My brain is fucked and I have nothing to say...The End.*

THREE

His bed was new. He was unable to sleep in their marital bed without her. He had thrown the old mattress in the back of his new pickup and escaped past the town's border, and lugged it into the murky water like a crime boss getting rid of his latest victim. He had stood on the riverbank, chugging from a bottle of whisky and snickered as it floated, gurgled and vanished before his eyes.

It was nearing the Witching Hour. His eyelids fluttered like a butterfly's wings, and he watched, helpless, as he walked along a reincarnated path that would lead him to his dead wife. He knew she would be at the end of the pass, and he didn't want to see her. He was enraged with the idea that she would only come at night, and he felt duped by a sardonic version of herself. This new courtship contaminated what they once shared, and as he brought himself out of sleep and shifted to his left side, he thought of that time that he first laid eyes on her:

April, 1966

I dream of doing it in exotic places,
I'd like to look up and see rafters,
Perhaps a sign that reads:
We Do Not Serve On A First Come, First Serve Basis, But By
Degree of Severty

"You spelled severity wrong."

He twisted his head to see the woman sitting next to him with a bloody bandage dressing her hand. His arm was in a make-shift sling until they could see him and tell him to keep it that way. His boss at the mill would have something to say about it on Monday, and Luke will wash colourful words over the guy until he'll retreat back into his hole, or pick on the new kid with the freckled face and dwarfed nose.

His scribble was illegible and he marvelled at the fact that she was able to decipher it. He grew cross that she had set eyes on his poetry. Not even his own ma was allowed to read that which was born of his subconscious, since she'd probably call on Doc Sprite to evaluate his diseased mind.

"Are you spying on me?"

"Look," she said, ignoring his question and pointing with her good hand, "you're missing the 'i', see?"

Luke stared at his pad and erased the offending word and re-wrote it as neatly as possible for his audience of one, "Better?" he asked her.

"You know it is. Why you askin'?"

"Askin'?"

She sneered at him, "Oh, I'm sorry. Let me rephrase that for you. Why are you asking me if it's better, if you already know that it is, asshole.*"*

He studied her face, bewildered by the smile that lingered on her lips that so easily spewed profanity.

"What happened to your hand?"

"Cut it making pasta."

"You Italian?" he asked her, hopeful.

"Yeah. You?"

"Yeah."

"Cool."

Her long, olive-toned legs were shaking underneath her white mini-skirt.

"Are you cold?"

"Hot as hell in here."

"Then why are you shaking?"

"Cuz it hurts," she said, raising her mummified hand in his direction. "What did you do to yourself?"

"Sledgehammer."

Her smile returned, "We're a clumsy pair, aren't we? So, exotic places, huh?"

He turned the notepad over on his knee and lit himself a smoke, distracting himself by watching new patients shuffle in to stand in line like they were entering hell's portal. One skeletal thin child moaned for relief, while his mother hushed him by feeding him cookies from a tin.

"Don't want to talk about it?"

He turned his head in her direction, feeling the blood rush to his groin. Her features were perfect like his stupid sister's porcelain dolls that still sit in their childhood home, lined on the windowsill, and put there to keep out would-be-suitors who never came.

"I like to write, so?"

"I can see that. I wasn't saying anything bad. What's your name?"

"Luciano. Luke."

"I'm Claudia."

He proved he was listening by blowing smoke in her face. He dropped it to his feet and crushed it. He was sick of waiting. His ass hurt from sitting for four hours.

"I gotta go," he told her, coming to his feet.

She stood quickly, "Where?"

"Tired of waiting."

"But what about your arm?"

"It'll heal. You coming?"

She looked around the hospital waiting room and instinctively covered her mouth to dispel the virus gods from foraging her body.

"I think I need stitches."

He swam in her pupils and then told her, "I got a bottle of whisky and a sewing needle at home."

She debated with the voice inside of her warning her that he could kill her once they were alone, and then she decided that murderers don't write sexy poetry.

"I'm comin'..."

Luke placed his feet on the freezing cold floor and walked through the house, intent to quiet the racket that was preventing him from sleeping. His eyes adjusted to the darkness that pervaded. The icy soles of his feet hurt, sending shock waves up his naked legs. He saw its outline as it shivered in one corner of the kitchen. Its eyes glowed through the blackness like that a mini-demon. He crouched to the floor and shot his hand out, swiftly taking it by the neck. He stood again, keeping it at arm's length and squeezed until the demon eyes mimicked his own fluttering lids. The tiny bleats made his ears bleed. He pulled a drawer open with one hand and searched for the butcher knife; the one he ordered Claudia not to use, lest she cut herself.

He imagined how they used to do it, in ancient times, underneath a blood red moon. He forced his arm to sweep the air, and they both looked away.

In an instant, silence filled the room.

The lamb's blood dripped on his toes, making them wiggle.

FOUR

Rain or shine, there were always shadows in his house. He loathed the sunlight and always kept the curtains closed. In the morning, Luke remembered his dream and his eyes ventured towards the corner of the kitchen where the slaughter took place. He prepped his coffee and walked to the living room to join his muse. He stared at the Remington, classifying it a sort of enemy. Instead, he brandished his pen and paper, hoping to elicit words from swirls of ink, but his muse had hung herself overnight and nothing but doodles and scribbles materialized on the pad.

He picked up the machine, feeling the weight of fictional worlds on his shoulders and walked over to Claudia's grandfather's desk that sat against one wall housing an empty vase, a decorative dish and a lamp. He turned on the lamp and it emitted just the perfect amount of light for his writing pleasure. He retrieved his coffee, sat down, cracked his knuckles, and poised his fingers over the keys, but all he saw was red.

He didn't run to the kitchen, nor did he panic in any sort of way, but he was strangely curious about the dot on the floor that was gracing the white tile in the form of a perfect little circle. He licked his finger and crouched down, smudging the burgundy dot until it turned crimson in colour. He stared at his own finger, and rubbed his thumb against it until the sight of the blood managed to mar his beliefs, forever colouring him as a dunce without the cap.

"Jesus fucking Christ."

The rest of the kitchen was void of any evidence, except that he could hear the echo of the tiny bleat. He placed both hands over his ears, spinning stupidly until vertigo had him meet the floor and he stayed there thinking that he was very quickly losing his mind.

FIVE

He poured more Whisky into his coffee mug and gulped it down, aware that it was dribbling down his chin. His trembling hands met the keys:

"The prognosis is not very good. We're going to have to remove his lassitude"

"Are you sure, Doctor?"

"He will have no place in our regime if we leave it in. Please inform the family."

The nurse waddled away, dragging her 8th arm. Her misshapen head bobbed side to side.

Luke shifted his body in the wooden chair and looked around the living room expecting to see an alien with four boobs, but he was alone with his own demented thoughts. He turned back to the typewriter:

Winter's gentle snow failed to cleanse him as he sat at the foot of her grave, telling her stories she could never hear...

He knocked his chair over and walked to his living room window. Pulling the drapes open by crooking one finger, he saw only a sprinkling of rain descend from a blackened sky.

"What the Christ is going on!?" His own voice startled him

into resigning to the fact that Mary's little lamb was still a one-dimensional creature on a crinkled sheet of paper. He walked over to the coffee table and picked it up, thinking that he would feel it vibrate beneath his fingers. He dropped it and watched it float back in its place.

In the bathroom, he stripped naked, and stepped into the shower, voluntarily scalding himself with hot water. He closed his eyes, adjusted the temperature and let the water comfort him like the arms of a woman comfort a man in distress. The warmth was soothing and he wrapped his arms around himself, hugging himself just like she used to embrace him. He could smell her sweet hair, chestnut brown and straight as an arrow. He could feel her breasts against his, and her fingertips inch perpetually down his back and to his backside; up and down and over and over again until her jealous lips would find him at attention and she would take him, greedily.

He was sick of thinking of her and lathered her away, and just as he betrayed her in his mind, the water turned icy cold so that he shot his eyes open and saw the tub begin to fill with millions of unique snowflakes, turning the bathroom into a veritable Winter Wonderland.

SIX

He sat outside, engaging the crickets by chirping back at them and rocked back and forth in the porch swing; whisky bottle in tow. After a while, he walked to his shed, found the proper tool and proceeded to saw the thing in half. He had built it for her on their third wedding anniversary and its incessant rocking produced a wrath that he recognized as the same feeling he harboured at her funeral when doting relatives tried to fill the hole in his heart by cooking a plethora of Italian delicacies.

He spewed ugly profanities into the night. His spittle mixed with the whisky, allowing the bugs, worms and birds to partake in a sort of happy hour. He threw the saw on the porch, clapped his hands together and headed inside, deciding that the deadbolts were useless against his supernatural guests.

He stumbled over his own two feet and cursed loudly, hoping to startle the ghosts into submission. At the typewriter, he typed furiously:

He offered her champagne kisses in the wake of their new status as husband and wife. Claudia wore a simple white sheath and flowers in her hair. His brown suit and royal blue tie brought out the colour of his eyes, she had told him, stripping him of the costume...

He squeezed his eyes shut, seeing the numbers before his eyes. When he reached sixty, he opened them and tried to focus on his surroundings which were absolutely familiar to him. His victory manifested itself with the scent of roses filling the air. They were taken from her mother's garden and adorned the small room where they had feasted on wedding fare.

Luke inhaled deeply, sensing something else beneath the roses. The succulent aroma of roast pork filled his living room. He remembered feeding Claudia her favourite fatty bits. She had licked his fingers, sucking on them discreetly, acting very unlike a virgin bride.

He left his place in front of the machine and walked methodically around the house. As he made his way from room to room searching for her likeness, he saw his father-in-law in his mind's eye and remembered the last time he spoke to her parents when they argued with him that his presence in their lives only served to remind them of their dead daughter. Her mother busied herself by wrapping sandwiches with the plastic wrap that never stuck, while her father stood guard in front of the cash register wordlessly rebuking Luke for being alive. Luke had slammed his foot through the diner window, making one fat trucker recoil, causing his *Mountain Dew* to soak his bib. He drove past the town limits and when that wasn't far enough, he drove further and further, until the diner became just a speck on the map and he vowed to never lay eyes on dear sweet dad again.

In the bedroom, he pulled on a black sweater, maneuvering it over the bottle of whisky that was still clutched in his hand, and walked back to the living room, where, without any rhyme or reason, Claudia occupied the wooden chair, wearing only her white sheath wedding dress.

SEVEN

The whisky pooled at his feet. Shards of glass decorated the hardwood. He rubbed at his eyes with two knuckles, and popped them open to see that she was still keeping his seat warm for him. She punched at a few random keys, making the Remington rattle out senseless verbiage.

She spoke to the typewriter when she asked him, "Why'd you bring me back?"

She had lost her wreath of flowers off the beaten path, and wore her hair straight, hiding behind it as she typed.

The same senseless malarky escaped Luke's lips, "Is that you, Claud?"

She twisted her head without raising it, making her look like an old woman with a spinal condition, "Who the hell else would be sitting here in a goddamn wedding dress?"

She stared at him with a crease between her perfectly manicured brows until she relaxed her forehead muscles, and forced her lips into a smile, which melted instantly into a frown.

She pushed herself away from the desk and walked over to him, stepping on the glass as if it were warm, soft, sand beneath her feet.

"Why?" she repeated, lifting her fingers to his face and stroking his cheek, his chin, and the length of his neck. She felt him tremble underneath her touch, "Poor baby," she cooed at him, "Come here," she said, whilst pulling his head into her breast.

He wept without shame, soaking the antique lace on her

dress. His drunken knees buckled and together, they descended to the floor, still holding each other, just as they last did.

"You shouldn't have done it."

He clutched at her with his nails, leaving little indents on her skin. She was warm, but no matter how long he searched, he could not find her heartbeat. He placed her underneath him, kissing her the way she liked to be kissed.

"Shouldn't a done what?" he asked, slurring.

"Brought me back," she answered between breaths.

"Why, baby?"

He pulled at his sweatpants and raised her dress, exposing her thighs, and as he let himself pretend that she was real, he felt her insides, where it was no longer warm, but cold like a refrigerator's belly. She grasped at his sweater, and then her touch became feather-light and her hands dissolved, just as she was dissolving, and the last thing he saw, was her lips as she spoke the words, "Because I will just die again..."

EIGHT

He ran with his bare feet pounding the asphalt until his heels bled. He ran until a group of troubled teenagers stopped what they were doing and stared at the man in black, racing down the city streets like God's breath was forcing him forward. He ran around the block three times, ran up his front steps, into his foyer and this time, barricaded himself inside. He opened every curtain and turned on every light. The broken bottle was gone and so was the smell of crackling pig.

At the typewriter, he pounded out the word, seeking relief:

whisky whisky

He went on an Easter egg hunt for booze and found exactly 24 bottles of whisky stacked at attention on his kitchen counter. He grabbed one, twisted the cap off and drank liberally. In the living room, he dialed Ricky's number.

The phone rang incessantly, and he imagined Rick ravaging Sandra's body which made him drink faster.

He stared at the soles of his war-torn feet. A tiny shard of glass winked at him and he used the tip of his ballpoint pen to gouge it out. It fell to the floor and he stared at the space where only moments earlier, Claudia lay exposed to his touch.

He lied down on the couch and thought of his Zia and

wondered how many signs he's missed over the years that she was a descendent of witches. She was betrothed once, to a man with only one hand. She had shown up to Easter dinner with slashes dancing across her hollow cheeks as if her cat, Dante, had turned rabid. Instead, they were put there by the man with the hook as he attempted to caress her. Luke had always found the story suspicious, especially since he later found the guy alone, in the shed, hunched provocatively over an empty demijohn.

He died suddenly in the middle of the night and Zia had him cremated and placed his ashes in her favourite ceramic pitcher. It was the one her own mother had used to slow cook beans over an open fire during the war when the patriarch of the family lied belly down with his rifle on the roof of the tiny house. In the end, all that was left of their love affair was his claw. It was eventually glued to a piece of wood and poised above her front door like a lucky horseshoe.

He stared at his empty ring finger and felt the words vibrate past his lips.

Since you've been gone, all that's left is a band of gold... *Since you've been gone, all that's left is a band of gold! Since you've been gone, all that's left is a BAND OF GOLD!!!!*

He lifted his weary body from the couch, looked up at the sky and cursed his wife.

"Fuck you, Claud!"

The keys beckoned him.

Do you remember the time we went hiking and you slipped? Do you remember me catching you before you could stumble to your death? Maybe you remember the damn cup of coffee I went to get seconds before your beautiful body became tangled with the harsh metal of the Ford? Stay where you are, Claudia, because I'm coming back to save you, just like that day on White Mountain when I saved you.

Horrified, he stared at the page.

"Jesus, no. No, no, *no!*"

He pounded his fist on the keys, so that they lifted simultaneously, mocking him like the crowd did at his first major ball game when he missed the goal post by a hair. The girls and boys had stood, booing and hissing at him, causing Coach Stevens to blow on his whistle until his cheeks puffed in anger.

He glanced at the clock and willed the second hand to slow down.

In the bedroom, he changed his clothes, locked the house, and jumped into his pick-up securing his bottle next to him with a click of the seat-belt. He neglected to fasten his own, and sped through town, intent to join her the old-fashioned way.

NINE

He walked the aisles of *Mortimer's Need & Feed*, scanning the shelves like a castaway searches the beach for fish carcasses. A grotesquely overweight woman followed him, pushing her overflowing cart with the squeaky wheels. He looked behind him and she smiled lipstick pink teeth at him.

He swayed drunkenly on his feet, feeling the sweat drip down one side of his face, making him scratch at it as if deep in thought.

A pizza-faced kid stacking cans of condensed soup, wearing the trademark red apron over his t-shirt addressed him with Mortimer's signature greeting.

"Welcome to our store, if there is anything I can help you find, we will fill the need to feed. Is there anything I can help you find today, sir?"

Luke waited while the woman rolled past them. She threw one last gruesome greeting at the handsome man who reminded her of Clark Gable, and ignored the kid who blatantly watched her massive buttocks bounce up and down in tandem with the elevator music blaring from a radio at the front of the store.

"Yeah. I need ink."

Pizza-face turned back to his customer, "Squid ink?"

Luke envisioned his fist flying into the kid's nose and saw the blood spray onto his pristine vest. Then he vaguely wondered if squid ink was in high demand.

"No. Typewriter ink," he told him, smelling the Whisky on the air before him.

"Oh, you have a *need*, then. That would be in our stationery section. Follow me."

They walked to the other side of the store, stopping along the way to help an elderly man reach a box of instant stuffing. The man thanked them each with a shiny new dime. Luke jiggled it in his jeans pocket, along with his car keys, and followed pizza-face like a lost puppy.

"You should find ink on this wall."

"Gee, thanks for your help."

"You're welcome," the kid proudly told him. He disappeared around the corner and into another aisle, to hunt for the 400 lb seductress of his dreams, planning to seduce her with Cream of Mushroom soup.

Luke stared at the wall in front of him; eyes bouncing left to right. His face hurt from the constant scratching. Finally, he found the reels of ink that looked identical to the dying ones at home, grabbed two packages and walked over to the cash registers. A long line of customers waited impatiently for their turn. He glanced at the carts that held enough food to feed the needs of a hundred people.

He tapped the shoulder of the woman in front of him, wishing he had a stick of gum.

"Yes?"

"Hi. I, uh, have only these two things," he said, holding up his hand. "Do you think maybe I can..."

"No," she stated bluntly, turning back around.

He eyed the delightfully pink butt of roast in the woman's cart and imagined its maggot-filled insides spewing all over her favourite dinnerware, wiggling vivaciously to a Vaudeville tune.

He tapped her shoulder thrice more, "Excuse me?"

"What do you want?" she asked him, spinning around. She was young; younger than him, and wore a string of pearls around her neck like his ninety-one year old nonna used to wear at weddings and funerals alike.

"It's an emergency and I'm in a hurry," he said dramatically, holding up his hand again, and wishing he could shove the reels directly up her nose.

The woman stared at his shaking fingers and then inched her cart forward with the line, ignoring the look of panic in Luke's dark eyes.

"Thank-you for your graciousness, your majesty," he mumbled, dropping his hand in defeat.

"Fuck you," she replied, talking to the old man's back in front of her, causing the senior to whack her knuckles with his cane.

"Owww!" she screamed.

Luke looked around him. The line at Checkout #3 was moving at an alarming pace. He left the carnage to unfold without him and squished past the shoppers who were waiting their turn, proudly joining the chosen ones at #3.

The teenage girl at the cash register was pushing items across the belt like a well-oiled machine. Luke gleefully watched her fingers dance, until suddenly, they froze in mid-air. An audible gasp emerged from the lungs of *Need & Feed* shoppers.

They watched in unison as the girl picked up the can without a label and turned it over in her hands. The shamed would-be owner of the mystery veggie, tried to hide their embarrassment behind a shy smile, apologizing by lifting both shoulders to the sky.

The teen hesitated, picked up her mic, and spoke the two dreaded words with consternation: "Price check!"

He felt the blood rush to his toes. "Oh, for fuck sakes!" Luke yelled; frantic. "Who the hell tries to buy a can with *no label!?*"

The princess in aisle four with the bruised knuckles smirked before showing him her long, lizard-like tongue. The itch at his temple grew worse. The crowd waited in anticipation. Pizza-face sauntered up to the cash sporting a very suspicious pink smear on his left cheek.

Luke shifted from foot to foot, cursing inwardly, until the devil breathed fire, making him play limbo with the chain securing a deserted Checkout #5. He joined the threesome at #3, threw a handful of change on the belt, and saluted an astonished pizza-face before telling him, "For the ink. Send Mort my regards."

In the parking lot, the whisky met his lips like an impatient lover.

TEN

Luke stared at his television set depicting a gent and his dame kissing passionately by platonically pressing their lips together. The woman's mouth looked black, as glorious technicolor had yet to make a debut.

He stretched his eyelids open with four fingers but succumbed to the whisky and dozed off in the middle of his Mortadella. Provolone, and pickled eggplant sandwich. In his dreams, he saw her saunter towards him with the same black mouth:

"Dinner is almost ready, darling," she told him, sitting on the arm of his favourite chair and crossing her legs with one black patent pump poised seductively in his line of vision.

He lowered his newspaper, "It smells delicious, Claudia. What are we having?"

"I'm making your favourite pot roast with all the trimmings."

"Marvelous," he told her, focusing his attention on the headlines.

"Well I never!"

He pulled the pipe from his lips, "You never what, darling?"

"I spend all day making your favourite meal and you don't even notice my new shoes!" she pouted, thrusting her foot further in his direction.

He lowered his paper to take a better look, "I'm sorry,

Claudia, they are very nice shoes. Did you buy them at the department store?"

"No, in fact. Old Mr. Hubbard gave me a groovy deal."

"That's swell," he told her throwing the newspaper on the floor and pulling her onto his lap.

"Luke! The pot roast!"

"It will be fine, don't you think?" he asked, kissing her neck.

She squealed and squirmed before melting into his strong arms.

"You do realize what today is?"

"Tuesday?"

"It's our wedding anniversary!"

"Of course it is, darling," he told her, pecking her cheek.

She jumped from his lap and stood before him, with both hands on her hips.

"Next I bet you are going to tell me that you hate pot roast!"

He rose from the chair and unbuttoned his suit jacket, "Don't be silly, Claudia, I love your pot roast."

"You do?"

"Of course I do. Can we stop this charade now and get to the point of the matter?"

A slight smiled formed on her lips, "What might that be?"

"That I want to fuck your brains out."

"Oh, Luke," she whispered, falling into him...

He jerked awake, feeling the vomit rise from his belly. In

the bathroom he heaved what little food lined his stomach, coughing and spitting out bits of Italian bologna. At the sink, he splashed cold water on his face, wishing to drown himself. He raised his head and forced a smile, loathing the sight of his own reflection.

He walked back to the living room to face his nemesis. He sat gingerly on the edge of his chair and tapped at a few keys for the hundredth time since replacing the reels, hoping that the dark black ink would transform the old Remington into a genie:

I want to hold you again like I used to hold you. I want to hear your laugh and see your smile. My wedding ring, I didn't see it as an endless circle of love, but more as the gaping hole in my heart that you were sent to fill. You wanted to go for a ride that day. You loved the rain. It brought you solace and comfort. You wanted to dance naked in it. You always were the devil in a dress. I want to come to you now but I'm afraid. I'm a coward. I...~~need more whisky.~~

ELEVEN

He was naked, save for his jeans. He had rummaged through his drawers and his closet to find the same pair he wore that day, splotched with bits of her blood. He shaved and applied her favourite cologne. It was the one she said reminded her of a lumberjack in a quiet wood on a snowy day. He looked down at himself, disgusted, and threw himself to the floor, struggling through thirty sit-ups and thirty push-ups. Taking one last gulp of booze, he wrote himself away:

"Where do you think you're going?"
Her hand reached for him, pulling him back down for a kiss.
"Just across the way, baby. Coffee."
"You're lucky my dad's not here tonight. Hurry," she ordered him, slapping at his bare chest.

Luke leaned back in his chair and closed his eyes, hearing the echo from the clanging of the keys fade away. He felt a drop on his face and then another and then hundreds of the same. He heard thunder roll though his living room and the blast of a car horn coming from the main road. He held his hands over his naked abs, clasping them tighter at the sound of people's chatter.

He sat up blind, slowly opening one eye and then the other until they adjusted to the darkness and he found himself sitting on the diner steps, staring at his old pick-up truck. The rain dripped down his face like streams of blood. He wiped at his cheeks with both hands, and stared at his unstained palms, enjoying the lyrical sound of his own laughter. He stood slowly, unsteadily, and walked towards his old Ford, picking up his pace to a jog and then finally, he ran to her.

Peering over the bed of the pick-up, he saw her smile up at him from where she lay like *Sleeping Beauty,* and when she spoke, her voice sent shock waves to his shattered heart.

"Forget something?"

"I...oh God..."

She sat up, hiding her naked breasts with her arms. "What is it? What's wrong?"

"Claud..."

"What!?"

He looked around the parking lot for signs of the transport that would take her life. He remembered the scene in the aftermath, watching as the driver stumbled from his cab and fell to his knees. He remembered his own body convulsing with sobs and scoffing at the man's plight as he, too, wept from regret. A crowd had gathered, as if standing at a concert, and they held their breath in unison at the sound of a siren drawing near. They had looked on as Luke pulled the man to his feet, and showed him Claudia's mangled remains until the trucker fell over from shock and welcomed the kicks to his head, that sent him to sleep.

Luke looked back at his wife, focusing on her cupid's bow and staring as she pulled his t-shirt up to her chest, and before she could speak, he asked her with as much conviction as his lungs would allow, "Do you want hot chocolate instead?"

"Jesus Christ, Luke, I don't care. Hurry up."

He nodded and held her chin beneath two fingers, kissing her warm, wet, lips, "I love you." He stroked her hair, turned around and ran back to the diner.

She shouted her admission of love through the rain and thunder and the roar of the night, but the three words were buried beneath the sound of the crash, along with the beat of his heart.

TWELVE

He paced his living room, admonishing himself by beating himself in the head with the whisky bottle. "Stupid Luke. Stupid, *stupid, stupid!!*" On impact, he was transported back to his house in a dizzying Dorothy-like fashion.

The shrill of the telephone forced him to pull the thing from the wall. He threw it on the couch, keeping whoever was on the other end at bay. He recalled a hot Summer's day when a long line of familial blood trotted up his driveway. They stood on his porch like a coven. The women dressed in black wrung their hands in worry, while the patriarchs came armed with their own horror stories from the war, ready to guilt Luke out of his mourning. His weight had plummeted to a mere 140 lbs. They stood above him while forcing him to consume a chicken soup that promised to "put hair on his chest". He pushed the bone marrow around his bowl, squishing it with the back of his spoon, marvelling at its sponginess. He placated the herd until they were satisfied that he wasn't going to kill himself. They left as a bunch and Luke retreated back into his shell, vowing to never again eat chicken soup.

He smoked his fifth cigarette in an hour, coughing up the effects of the over-indulgence until he spat on his own floor. He pulled on a t-shirt and then sat down at the desk, ready to rumble:

You ordered eggs for dinner and did that thing of yours

that made you look so sexy. You stuffed the entire yolk in your mouth, letting the gooey mess slide down your throat as if savouring the world's most expensive caviar...

"More coffee?"

Luke sat across from her, holding his turkey bacon club sandwich in mid-air.

"Luke? She asked if you want coffee."

"Uh...yeah," he said, sliding the thick ceramic cup towards the waitress.

"Thanks, Cathy," Claudia told the woman.

"Don't sweat it. Say, my ma wants to play Bingo this Saturday with your ma. Can you ask her?"

"Yeah. I'm sure she'll bring all her pennies."

"Great, thanks. Enjoy dinner you two."

She walked away, swatting at Joe Hadley's hand before it could violate her pear-shaped ass.

"How's the grub?"

Underneath the lights of the diner, Claudia was unlike a dream and was simply *there.* Her half-eaten plate proved she was three-dimensional. She smoked a mid-meal cigarette and stared at him with a twist in her smile.

He looked around him, amazed that everything was an exact replica of the night his heart died, right down to the teenagers causing a ruckus, and the smell of bacon grease perfuming the air.

"Luke? The sandwich?"

He focused his eyes on her, "It's...fine."

"Fine? You love turkey club. Are you okay?"

"Yeah," he said, placing his food on his plate, "listen, Claud, do you want to go home?"

"Home? We just got here. I'm not even done eating," she replied, snuffing out her smoke. She picked up her fork and pierced three fated home fries. "Are you sick?"

"Sick in love."

She shook her head at him, "Writerly you is showing."

He snatched at her free hand like a crocodile does its prey, "I mean it, Claud. I love you. You know that, right?"

"What the hell has gotten into you?" she asked him, squeezing his hand tenderly.

"Tell me that you know," he ordered, desperate.

"Of course I know! See?" she said, holding up her hand and showing him her wedding ring.

His breath escaped his lungs. "Then come home with me."

"But it's starting to sprinkle. Please, Luke? Just a while longer. I can make it worth your while," she told him suggestively.

He felt her foot slide up his jeans. Despite the horror-show he was living in, he felt his insides awaken.

"What does that mean?"

"You know," she said, cocking her head towards their pick-up parked outside.

He faced the window and saw the invisible transport kissing their truck. "No."

"What?"

"I said no."

She leaned back against the booth and crossed her arms over her heart, "What the fuck, Luke?"

He saw the tears well in her eyes, unable to dab at them with fake words. "I just...trust me, Claudia."

"Trust you!? About what?"

"Goddammit," he mumbled. He picked up the cigarette package and lit himself a smoke, wishing he could burn along with it.

The teenagers in the booth behind them turned it up a notch. They were arguing about the merits of the prom queen's nether region in graphic detail. Claudia turned her body towards them, 'Shut the fuck up, would you?"

"Make us," one not-so-clever teen replied.

"Oh, I'll make you all right." She swung one leg out to exit the booth.

"Claud, stop."

"Why?"

Luke produced a ten dollar bill from his wallet and left in on the sticky table. He got up, took her hand and pulled her out the door like a father would a spoiled child, ignoring the teen boys' eyes as they ravaged his wife.

"Where are we going!?"

"The truck," he told her, throwing his smoke to the ground. "like you wanted. We should move it, though, okay?"

"I don't care where. Sure. Thank-you, Luke."

He kissed her in her hair. They both climbed into the Ford and he drove behind the building, parking in a spot safe from view, and safe from the ill-fated transport. He turned off the engine and grasped her hand, pulling her delicately towards him as if she would evaporate before his eyes. She leaned into him, and stiffened just as quickly, "My purse! I forgot my purse."

"My fault. Sorry, baby. I'll go."

"No. Let me. Too much coffee," she admitted, smiling.

The sweat beaded his forehead with dots of anxiety. He watched as she opened her door and descended from the cab. She walked over to his side of the truck and knocked on his window, requesting permission. He removed the barrier between them, and she kissed him before turning from him and yelling behind her, "I love you! Be right back!"

The rain was more of a mist, showering everything with an annoying spray. He stared as she disappeared around the corner of the building, leaving only her shadow behind. It stretched along the pavement, growing thinner and more sinister. Luke stared out the front windshield. He could see it from his peripheral vision as it came into view, nose first, veering and swerving after hitting the speed bump of human flesh and bones. The crunch was prevalent beneath his scream.

THIRTEEN

He stared at his blackened fingers. He had torn the ribbon from the machine, analyzing it and seeking answers. It lay next to the typewriter like a dead organ, surgically removed from its innards.

The sun slept, making room for a playful moon. His insides lurched. In the bathroom, he slammed the door shut and waited to purge. Thoughts of her singed every part of him. His limbs were as weak as his tattered brain. He let her die again, and for this sin, there was no penance great enough. He was making friends with satan.

At the sink, he washed the ink away and the diluted spots reminded him of a different time, when life held meaning:

"Quit pacing!"

He walked back and forth in front of her like an impatient father-to-be. There were only four chapters, but he was already hooked, and felt that thrill a writer seeks when they wake every morning, ready to create magic.

"Sorry, baby, but what's taking you so long!?"

She didn't look up at him when she held one finger in the air, asking him for another painstaking minute. He stared, horrified, as the tears fell, plopping on his manuscript and destroying a single word.

"Oh God, that bad?"

She lifted her head slowly, shaking it back and forth, "No, baby. Not bad. Brilliant."

He beamed. "Yeah!?

"Yeah," she said, patting the spot on the couch next to her.

He sat, unable to stop his leg from bouncing up and down. She rested her hand on it and he felt heat emanate from her palm, sending a surge of love to his very core.

"I love it, Luke."

"It needs some work, but..."

"Nah. Don't touch a single word."

He scrunched his hair in his fingers, grinning like a school-boy in lust with his first crush.

"Do you like the premise?"

"The what?"

"The story line."

She nodded, "Especially this part," she told him, flipping pages and scanning each paragraph.

"Which one?"

"Hang on, I'm lookin'."

"Well look faster!"

"Here," she finally said, releasing him from his misery. She read out loud, "A biking accident shattered his left knee and he hung up his tap shoes. For years he could hear the fanciful rhythm in his dreams. At 98, he put them on again and danced one last time. His epitaph was scripted in Morse code."

The words sounded operatic on her lips.

"I just added that this morning. I'm glad you like it."

"I'm so proud of you," she said with a hint of melancholy.

"You are?"

She shook her hand out of her daze, "Of course I am! When do you plan to finish?"

He lit a victory smoke and handed it to her. Lighting his own, he told her, "A few weeks, I think."

"That's fast!"

"Yeah. Maybe a bit longer. Whatever it takes, I guess."

She crossed her naked legs, and pulled nervously at his t-shirt. The one she was wearing, "I wish I had a talent," she admitted. She avoided his eyes and stared at the emerald green carpeting. She imagined that it was lush green grass, and that a worm was nestled somewhere, sleeping.

"Hey...hey, look at me, baby," he pleaded, taking the manuscript that rested in her lap. He threw it on the coffee table so that the stapled sheets fluttered like the hem of a woman's dress caught in a gentle breeze.

"Claudia," he urged.

She lifted her head and met his eyes, feeling his hand encircle her wrist.

"You are amazing, baby. You do have talent. I mean, no one can make a tiramisu like yours."

"That's just baking," she said, puffing on her smoke.

"No. No, it's not. Remember my Zia Concetta's masterpiece at Christmas? Eh?" he repeated, forcing her to smile.

"You mean the rock hard cookies that broke Zio's dentures?"

"Yeah, those," he said, chuckling at the memory. The family had halted Yuletide celebrations in order to stop the old married couple from killing one another. "Besides," he continued, "you are amazing in so many other ways."

"Like what?" she asked, extinguishing her cigarette.

He pulled the hair from her face and tucked it behind her ear. "Like the way you make me feel," he told her, placing her hand on his heart. "And the way you love," he said, placing her fingertips on his lips. "And like the fact that you are the most amazing wife in the history of the world..." he trailed off, rubbing gently at her wedding ring.

Her eyes glistened. She teased him, "Are you trying to get laid, Luciano?"

"When am I not *trying* to get laid?"

They dissolved in laughter and she leaned into his shoulder and bit at it playfully. He whispered in her hair, "But I meant every single word, baby."

"Thank-you," she whispered back. After a minute, she raised her voice, "Luke?"

"Yeah?"

"Am I in your book?"

"Do you want to be?"

She sat up and stared at him, contemplating, "Not really. Ma might have a heart attack if there are any naked scenes."

He grinned at her child-like demeanor, "How about I dedicate it to you? I was going to anyway."

She nodded vigorously, "That would make me happy."

"Good. Now let's go," he said standing and pulling her by

the hand.

> *"Where?"*
>
> *"The place where dreams are made."*
>
> *She raised her eyebrows at him, "The bedroom?"*
>
> *"Nah. The kitchen..."*

He had eaten twice that night, savouring her for dessert.

He bit at his bottom lip until it bled. The memory was palpable, intermingling with her phantom kiss and making his mouth tingle with a desire so fierce, that he felt like a conjoined twin suddenly separated from its other half.

He battled with the bathroom door until it opened, and walked down the darkened hallway, pausing in front of a likeness of Jesus. Claudia's Nonna had insisted they hang the religious relic in their home to ward off evil spirits and to wash away the memories of those who lived in the house before them as if serial killers had inhabited the home. He played peek-a-boo with the Son of God for a while, and then he asked Him the question that has haunted him since her death.

> "Why not me? *Eh!?*"

The silence was deafening. He could hear the wind whip through the trees from an open window, and the sound of dogs mating in the neighbours yard.

> *"Well!?* Aren't you supposed to know it all!?"

He punched at the wall, missing Christ's chin by a mere inch. In the foyer, he struggled with his shoes and stuffed his arms in his varsity football jacket, found his car keys, and raced across town to seek advice from the only person who could shut up long enough to listen to the ramblings of a psychopath.

"*I said, and so it was,*" reverberated through an empty house.

FOURTEEN

In the truck, Gary Puckett whispered through the radio. Luke turned up the volume to hear Gary scream, in an attempt to vanquish his tortured thoughts. Uncle Vinny had beguiled them with the song that made Claudia blush. The lyrics to "Lady Willpower" had been lost on them, since they had already engaged in a rendezvous before the nuptials took place. Vinny's orange striped suit transformed Claudia's uncle into a wedding singer for the night. His dream had always been to sing in Vegas, like those Elvis impersonators in the tacky chapels. He lived the dream for a night, and died the next morning after his drunken stupor helped propel him from a five-story balcony. Luke's mother surmised that it wasn't Vinny's love of Sambuca that sent him over the edge, but the fact that he lived at 17 Constance Drive, giving life to the superstition that the innocent number in roman numerals translates to "I have lived".

"He lived too much!" she had shouted at his wake.

In a last toast to the lush, Luke raised the whisky bottle before an open road, "To you, Vinny. *Vai con Dio.*"

He pulled up to the black wrought iron gate that graced the entrance to *Woodlawn Cemetery.* He looked up, expecting to see a full moon, but it was merely a sliver. He pulled the collar of his jacket around his ears and trekked through the grounds, trying to remember where she rested. The only sound that resounded from his intrusion was that of the whisky sloshing in the half-empty bottle. He never visited her. He found the notion ridiculous and scoffed at the idea that she would somehow sense his worldly presence.

He cursed himself for forgetting a flashlight. The space was endless, lined with rows upon rows of weathered headstones of various sizes and colours, commemorating forgotten ones. Other monuments were adorned with fresh bouquets of flowers or pictures of loved ones partaking in a pretend tea with the deceased.

He crossed himself, to thwart the advances of dead prostitutes or spinsters, turned spectres. He imagined their skeletal remains plunging above earth to tackle him and violate his very warm flesh and blood. He laughed out loud at the thought of an overly jealous Claudia engaging in a cat fight with the ghosts, like the time she had pinched Carla Ronetti's arm for grabbing a handful of Luke's ass at a house party. The slut had sported a bruise for weeks, claiming she had a run-in with her ex-boyfriend. Her brothers had searched for Marco Cavenelli high and low, and beat the hell out of him one night until Carla fessed up. The brothers had bruised her opposite arm for her and she eventually ran away to a Nunnery of the Shakespearean variety.

Luke froze. A man's voice drifted towards him. His laugh had alerted the grave robber that he wasn't not alone. He stopped dead in his tracks and wondered if the bottle clutched in his hand could serve to protect him or if he should tame the beast by offering him a drink.

A second man's voice danced on the air, followed by a third. He moved only his eyes in search of the hoodlums but saw nothing. He was cloaked in darkness but unable to move, should the sound of leaves crunching beneath his feet give him away.

His demise was imminent and he hoped that whoever found him in the morning, raped and pillaged, would think to lay his corpse next to his wife.

Three extremely perverted looking shapes walked towards him. They emerged out of the shadows wielding leaf endowed tree branches as weapons, as if meaning to tickle someone to death.

"Well, looky here..." the biggest of the three said in introduction. "We got ourselves a live one boys."

"Howdy," Luke told them all, calling on his Sunday-school manners.

Sloth 2 gurgled something in reply, while sloth number 3 desecrated one poor man's grave by spitting on it. Their eyes shone red through the darkness, advertising their previous exploits with booze or drugs or, likely, both.

"Let's make this short and sweet, shall we?"

Luke pulled from his bottle and shoved it at Big Guy who took it greedily.

"Are we done here?" Luke asked.

"Not even close," Big Guy said, ignoring the whisky cascading down his square chin. "Money."

"Money?"

"You deaf?" Sloth 3 asked.

"Not likely, since I just repeated the word."

Sloth 2 chimed in with little wit, "Wise guy, eh?"

"Sometimes. Sometimes I'm a victim of my own circumstances."

"What the fuck are you talking about? Just give us your

wallet," Big Guy retorted impatiently.

"Wallet?"

"Of for fuck sake's," Sloth 2 and 3 said in unison. They moved forward, ready to stop with the pleasantries.

"Wait," Luke said, pushing his hand out in defence. He reached in his back jeans' pocket for his wallet and produced it like a magician and his rabbit. "Here, see?"

"Yeah, we see. Hand it over."

"One moment, sir. Behold," he said channelling Houdini.

"What's with this guy?" one bloke mumbled, addressing his friends.

Luke opened the wallet and showed them its vacant contents. "I'm broke."

They all three stared into the leather money holder and then looked at each other and shrugged.

"That's too bad."

"Yes," Luke said, placing it back in his jeans. "It is quite unfortunate."

Big Guy gulped from the bottle and then placed it on a weathered tombstone. "Unfortunate for you."

"Quite," Luke said, before being tackled by the group.

His varsity football training did little to help him escape the onslaught. Their weight and size and girth overpowered his modest frame. He lay underneath one mammoth, gagging at his special blend of body odour. He accepted a few punches to his ribs from another member of the gang, while a third molested him by searching his body for something of value.

"Come on, Dick, he's worthless," he heard one say. The

crowd dispersed and came to their feet.

Luke erupted in a fit of painful laughter, holding his side, and coughing uncontrollably.

"What the fuck is funny?"

"Nothing, *Dick*," he managed to say from his fetal position on the wet grass.

Silence preceded the hypothetical question, "You think my name is funny?"

Luke remained quiet, laughing beneath his breath and trying to focus through one eye that was swelling like a boxer's after a title win.

"Here that boys?" Dick asked his clan. "He thinks my name is funny."

"That's terrible, boss."

"Yeah, terrible, boss."

They beat at him with their tree branches making him feel like Julius Caesar being fanned and fed, and fawned upon by a splendiferous hive of half-naked women.

Luke laughed harder, and then his world went black.

FIFTEEN

The pounding in his head escalated to jack-hammer proportions. He managed to crawl his way back to his pick-up, slithering on his belly. His unscathed legs worked fine, but he was dejected; done, and wanted to see life as the vermin did.

The pounding grew louder and then he heard her familiar voice accompany the hammering.

"Luciano! Are you in there? Your truck is here! It's ma!"

He finished replacing the ribbon in the machine, got up, and peeked through his front window curtains, as if to ensure that his mother was not simply a figment of his imagination.

He unlocked the front door and pulled it open, mentally preparing himself for her meltdown.

"Dio mio! What the hell happened to you?"

She let herself in and placed whatever was hiding in the foil pan on the floor. She pulled a tissue from inside her shirt sleeve, licked it, and wiped at her grown son's face where dirt and blood lingered as evidence of his jaunt through the cemetery.

"I fell," he said, scrunching his face like a two-year old.

"On a fist!? Look at your eye!"

"I can't see my own eye, ma."

"Don't be smart! Here," she said, bending over and picking up the pan, "I made you cannelloni. With spinach and ricotta." She thrust the pan in his arms and walked to the living room where the telephone still sat on the couch, "No wonder you don't answer the phone! I've been calling you, you know."

"Sorry, ma," he yelled from the kitchen. He kept his head in the fridge for a full minute to cool down and to try and wake himself from his stupor.

He found her sitting with her hands in her lap, teetering on the edge of the couch like she always did. *"To save the fabric."*

"So what's wrong with you? What happened?"

"Nothing," he told her, fully aware that his lie would only make her more suspicious.

"I don't believe you, Luciano," she said, reading his thoughts. "Why haven't you come by? Your father thinks you have a new girlfriend. Is that true?"

"Why do you have to say shit like that?"

"Like what? And don't swear!"

Her stout, round frame was reminiscent of a marshmallow. She wore her greying hair in tight little curls. A gold medallion featuring *La Madonna* rested between her breasts. She held the chain, seeking comfort and guidance, just like the time when Luke was six, and had broken his ankle at the playground. He had been imprisoned on the merry-go-round for hours. The family had set out to look for him, sans pitchforks, and when they finally found him, wailing like a little girl, his mother had kissed her necklace before she kissed him.

He sat next to her and lit a smoke. "I'm fine."

"Liar. Did you eat?"

"I had a sandwich."

"That's not enough. Thank the good Lord that I cooked all day. Your father doesn't even like spinach."

Luke twisted his body to face her, "How is Pop?"

She shrugged, "*Meh.* Same as usual. His arthritis is acting up again. Put on a few pounds."

He nodded and stared in front of him, watching the smoke twirl like a legless dancer.

"I'm worried about you. Why didn't you come to the funeral? Ricky was there."

He looked at her, remembering all the times she sat by his bedside to keep the monsters at bay. Her eyes were telling, lined with deep wrinkles. He felt like he owed her for all the sleepless nights spent agonizing over make-believe ghouls. He wanted to settle that debt, and tell her that the true terror is that which plagues him during his waking hours.

"Can I ask you something about her, ma?"

"What?"

"Was Zia a witch?"

She stuffed one finger in his face, "You don't get a slap only because you're already beat up!" She lowered her finger and clasped her hands together again, "What kind of question is that? You been doing the mary-wanna again?"

"Nah, ma. I just...never mind."

"Tell me!"

"Claudia..."

His mother immediately crossed herself and kissed the Virgin Mary, "What about her?"

"I've...been seeing her lately."

"Her ghost?" she asked without alarm, tucking the Mother of God back between her breasts.

"Why do you say it like that? Do you believe in ghosts?"

"I saw one. I thought I told you this story."

He crushed out his smoke and lit another, "No, you didn't."

"I didn't? Who did I tell then? Your Zio Alberto? Who cares, doesn't matter who. I saw my Nonno after he died. I was just a girl. Ten, eleven, maybe. Oh! I know who I told, it was..."

Luke struggled to keep his patience in line, "Ma, focus. What happened when you saw him?"

"Well, let's see. It was the middle of the night. I had to use the bathroom. He died the previous day but he was in Italy, so I never met him in real life."

"But you knew it was him?"

"Of course I knew it was him. His picture was all over the house. Anyway, it was dark. I couldn't see my own hand in front of my face and heard a whisper. I thought it was your Zia Monica playing around with me, but it was a man's voice. So I turned around and there he was. He was wearing a black suit and hat and smiled at me. He sort of glowed like your sister when she wears too much powder on her face."

"Well, what did he say?" he asked her, extinguishing his half-smoked cigarette.

His mother stood and brushed at her powder blue slacks. "He said, *'Hi, little one. Remember to never put off for tomorrow what you can do today.'* In Italian, of course."

"That's weird. Then what?" Luke asked her, following her to the foyer.

"Then nothing. He disappeared."

"So that was it?"

"Yeah. Listen, if you're seeing Claudia – may she rest in

peace – don't be afraid of her. She's still your wife." She patted at her son's heart and turned to leave.

Luke felt a sudden urge to nestle himself in bed, with his mother as guardian against the galaxy.

"I love you, ma."

She turned abruptly, "What does that mean?"

"Nothing. It means that I love you."

"Are you sick!?"

"What? No, ma, I just *love you.* Oh, forget it."

"Are you dying?"

"No."

"In trouble?"

"No, ma."

"Oh. Well, in that case, I love you too. Go eat."

He opened the door for her and watched as she descended his front steps and walked to her rusted, white Pontiac.

"Don't forget to eat!" she repeated, before driving away.

He waved at her and closed the door, securing it tightly against intruders; real and imagined.

He threw himself on the couch. He fought desperately, but eventually succumbed to a deep sleep. In his dreams, he heard the clanging of the keys, tapping endlessly in a realm far removed from his own.

An hour later, he woke to find a single word bleeding down the page: *Hurry.*

SIXTEEN

His house seemed to creak and groan. He could see his breath before him and he shivered from fright, sensing something wicked flow through him. His insides cried. He was starved for love.

There was a time when he was able to claim that he was content with his life. She had been his angel; his gift from God. They had dreams, like every young married couple. They had started to make plans to turn the spare bedrooms into nurseries, complete with pink and blue elephants strutting across the wallpaper. They wanted a plethora of kids sporting her dimpled cheeks and adopting his eyes. She said she wanted them to be artists, like him. She had spilled her guts one day, in bed, on a lazy Sunday afternoon. She had told him about her greatest fear that until then, stayed hidden within the confines of her mind. She was afraid that they couldn't conceive the natural way. He had smoothed her hair and kissed her tears away, telling her that if that were to happen, they still had each other and that they would find a way.

They made love tenderly that afternoon, aware of the fragility of life, and easing into the notion that the dream could shatter. They showered together under a warm spray. Her tears mingled with the water, and trickled down her lithe frame, washing down the drain; momentarily forgotten.

He purged his own thoughts with a last swig of the bottle and made his way to the bedroom where he stared at his reflection in the dresser mirror. He saw her standing behind him. She was whole and beautiful and when he turned to take her in his arms, she vanished, waiting for him in a different dimension.

He walked back to the living room, hunchbacked, and sat at the desk. His fingers itched. He poised them over the letters, unable to tame his trembling hands. He sat on them, raised them again over the Remington, and through the power of sheer, unadulterated love, he began to type:

April, 1966

I dream of doing it in exotic places,
I'd like to look up and see rafters,
Perhaps a sign that reads:
We Do Not Serve On A First Come, First Serve Basis, But By
Degree of Severty

He closed his eyes and counted to sixty. He heard a doctor being summoned over the loud speaker. He overheard a patient discussing his case with a nurse. He winced at the noise of beeping machines, and a telephone ringing, and when he opened his eyes at the sound of her voice, his heart soared into his throat.

"You spelled severity wrong."
He twisted his head to see his wife sitting next to him with a bloody bandage dressing her hand.
He struggled to speak, and could hear his own heart

beating, and could feel it throbbing at his pulse points.

"Are you spying on me?"

"Look," she said, ignoring his question and pointing with her good hand, "you're missing the 'i', see?"

She was ethereal and exuded sexiness by simply sitting there.

"I see," he said, with the type of shy smile he reserved for strangers.

She frowned at him, like a million times before, "You didn't even look."

He stared at her without blinking.

"What the hell you lookin' at?" she asked him, nervously.

"It's just..."

"Just what? You some sort of creep or something?"

He grinned internally, "No. You're just ridiculously beautiful."

"Come on," she said, blushing.

"I mean it."

"Well, thank-you. Is a hospital waiting room your usual place to pick up women?"

"What happened to your hand?" he asked her, changing the subject.

"Cut it making pasta. What about you?" She raised her good hand and feathered her fingers across his bruised cheek.

"Bar fight."

"Tough guy, eh?"

"They were."

They laughed together and he memorized the pitch of her

voice and the smile lines that captured her spirit and illustrated the love in her heart. As the echo died, he spewed more lies.

"I gotta go," he managed to say, coming to his feet.

She stood quickly, "Where?"

"Tired of waiting."

"But what about the doctor?"

"I'll heal," he said, fighting against the tears. "Take care of yourself."

"You just goin' to leave?"

He clutched his pad to his chest to prevent her from seeing his heart crumbling into a million little pieces. "Yeah."

"Well, how about a drink this week?" she asked him bravely. He saw their entire life in her eyes. He wanted to take her hand and run with her to somewhere safe, remote, and towards salvation.

His words almost died on his lips, "I have a girlfriend."

"Oh. Lucky chick," she told him, sitting back down.

He looked at her as the woman he vowed to love forever. His eyes were glued to her. His feet were grounded, and then he heard the hideous sound of the transport crashing into their Ford, and he willed himself to move.

"Here," he said, tearing the sheet off the notepad. "Souvenir."

She took it willingly and glanced at it before handing it back to him. "Will you sign it for me? In case you become some famous poet one day?"

"Sure."

He scribbled something at the bottom using an imposter's

handwriting and handed the sheet back to her. He forced his aching legs to turn from her, and made his way down the long, sanitized hallway like a dead-man walking. He didn't look back.

Alone, she stared at the inscription: *"Wingless angels, abound. All the best, Paul."*

SEVENTEEN

He was in agony. He sat on the carpet with his back against the couch, weeping into his knees. His entire body convulsed from his sobs. He used his remaining strength to scream into the void until his voice grew hoarse. The syllables teased him and tickled his lips, but he refused to say her name, lest she hear him - and he simply whispered, *Ti amo.*

He stood, but the weight of his reality forced him on the couch. He sat there, with his head back, welcoming the excruciating pain that he hoped would send him straight to hell.

Minutes passed like hours. He turned to look at it and then walked with it to the wall and plugged it back in. He turned the rotary dial, pausing at length before dialing the last number.

He wiped at his face with his shirt hem, and coughed away the angst.

"Hello?"

Sinatra blared in the background.

"Hi...is...is Claudia there?"

He waited for his mother-in-law to tell him that he was a failure; a loser, but instead, she said with a dubious tone in her voice in an attempt to dissuade her daughter's would-be-beau, "She's at work. Who's calling?"

"She's at work?"

"That's what I said. Who is..."

He hung up and tossed the phone back on the couch so that the receiver separated from its base, mocking him.

His breath escaped in one long exhale. He would remember her. In his mind, he would forever be her husband. In his heart, their love would be immortalized like words scripted in ink.

At the desk, he replaced the paper and scrolled to somewhere in the middle. The blank sheet was like a portal to his brave new world. He could journey to strange lands, and visit with warlords or mobsters. He could play the villain, detested by many or the hero, loved by all. He could even give her a different name and visit her sometime in the future or the distant past, or take her away on a starry ride to alien planets. He could travel back in time, before the day that he first laid eyes on her in the hospital, and see her savouring a Cappuccino, through a cafe window, somewhere in Paris or Italy. Strokes of his pen could possibly lead them to meet as children, choosing sides in the playground for Red Rover. He imagined pulling at her pigtails until years later, she would grow privy to his crush. They could share a single beer and explore each other's teenage bodies, masked beneath the roof of his father's car at the Drive-in. He could even once again bequeath his heart to her at the sacred altar.

He was a story-teller. He was the author of his own story, and as he caressed the keys like a lover does his lady, he realized that their story demanded only two more words...

...The End

Books by Barbara Avon

Peter Travis Love Stories:

My Love is Deep

Briana's Bistro

The Christmas Ornament

The Christmas Miracle

A Two-Part Love/Time Travel Story:

The Christmas Store

The Promise

Romance/Suspense/Time Travel:

STATIC

Romance/Thriller:

THE GIFT

Michael's Choice

Horror:

The Simpleton

SPEED BUMP

Q.W.E.R.T.Y

About the Author

Barbara Avon was born in Switzerland and came to Canada when she was two years old. She grew up Italian in the Niagara Region and attended Notre Dame High School, and then Brock University. She moved to Ottawa, Ontario, in 1999 to pursue work. She has worked for two major Ottawa area magazines and is a published poet.

Always having had a penchant for the written word, she has dreamed of writing a novel. "Q.W.E.R.T.Y", is her twelfth. She is working on her next novel, a love story with her characteristic suspense element.

In 2018, she won SpillWords Author of the Month, as well as FACES Magazine "Favourite Female Author".

Together with her husband, she has established BUCCILLI Publishing in homage to her maiden name.

She lives in Ontario, Canada with her husband Danny, their tarantula, Betsy and their houseplant, "Romeo".

34401816R00039

Made in the USA
Lexington, KY
22 March 2019